Get Lost!

D1486640

For my swimming buddies,
Marie and Cathy—N.K.

Text copyright © 2003 by Nancy Krulik. Illustrations copyright ©
2003 by John and Wendy. All rights reserved. Published by Grosset
& Dunlap, a division of Penguin Putnam Books for Young
Readers, 345 Hudson Street, New York, NY, 10014. GROSSET &
DUNLAP is a trademark of Penguin Putnam Inc. Published simul-
taneously in Canada. Printed in U.S.A.

Library of Congress Cataloging-in-Publication Data

Krulik, Nancy E.
Get lost! / by Nancy Krulik ; illustrated by John & Wendy.
p. cm.—(Katie Kazoo, switcheroo ; 6)
Summary: Katie Carew's third–grade class spends three days at
Science Camp, where Katie magically changes places with the
strict Head Counselor while on a hike and gets her group hope-
lessly lost. Includes directions for making all–natural soap.
[1. Camps—Fiction. 2. Camp counselors—Fiction. 3. Magic—
Fiction. 4. Lost children—Fiction.]   I. John, ill. II. Wendy, ill.
III. Title. IV. Series: Krulik, Nancy E. Katie Kazoo, switcheroo ; 6.
PZ7.K944Ge 2003
[Fic]—dc21
2002015624

ISBN 0-448-43101-7   H I J

Get Lost!

by Nancy Krulik • illustrated by John & Wendy

Grosset & Dunlap

Chapter 1

Katie Carew bent down and kissed her cocker spaniel on the nose. "Don't be afraid, Pepper," she told him. "I'm not going away forever. It's just three days."

Pepper sniffed at Katie's mouth. Then he licked her—right on the lips.

Katie let out a big yawn. It was 7:30 Monday morning. Usually, that was the time Katie got out of bed. But not today. Today Katie had already eaten breakfast. She was already dressed. And she was already at school!

Katie yawned again. She was so tired. She hadn't slept at all the night before. She'd been too nervous. She was about to go away to Science Camp—*for three days and two nights!*

Just then, a big yellow school bus pulled into the parking lot.

"Yahoo! The bus is here!" Manny Gonzalez shouted excitedly. "Science Camp, here we come!"

Katie's class had been talking about Science Camp since the first day of school. The third grade made the trip every year.

Some kids were really excited to go. Katie was more nervous. She had never been away from her family for that long before.

"Hey Katie, are you psyched or what?" Katie's best friend Jeremy Fox called out, as he and his mother walked onto the school playground.

"Or what," Katie answered nervously.

"Come on. Camp is great! I spent two weeks at sleepaway camp last summer. It was the best time of my whole life."

Jeremy was wearing hiking boots and

carrying a water canteen. He'd packed his clothes in a waterproof camp duffel bag. His sleeping bag was made of camouflage material.

Katie was wearing her everyday sneakers. Her mother had packed her clothes in the beat-up suitcase she used when she visited her grandma. Suddenly, Katie's Cuddle Bears sleeping bag seemed kind of babyish.

Katie's mom gave her a big squeeze. "You're going to have a great time. It's only two nights. Think of it as a long sleepover." Mrs. Carew pointed toward the edge of the playground. "Oh, look—here comes Suzanne!"

Suzanne Lock was Katie's other best friend. Katie figured she must have been planning for a *really* long sleepover. After all, she was wheeling a *huge* hot pink suitcase and carrying a small overnight bag. Her father was carrying the matching duffel bag.

Quickly, Katie hurried over to help Suzanne with her bags.

"Why do you have so much stuff?" Katie asked as she took the overnight bag from her friend. It was very heavy.

"A girl's got to be prepared for anything, Katie." Suzanne smiled as she unloaded the rest of her luggage beside Katie's. "If it's cold at night, I'll need a jacket. If it's warm during the day, I'll need shorts. And I don't want to wear the same outfit at night that I wore all day, so . . . ."

"We're going *camping!*" Jeremy shouted. "You're supposed to rough it!"

"I am! I didn't bring my blow-dryer."

Katie giggled. She was scared to go to Science Camp, but she was glad her two best friends would be there with her. She loved them both—even if they didn't always like each other.

"Hey, Katie, have you seen George?" Kevin Camilleri asked as he came running over. "Manny and I have to talk to him."

"I don't think he's here yet," Katie told him. "What's so important?"

"It's a secret," Kevin said. "We aren't telling anyone but George."

Just then, Mrs. Derkman stepped onto the playground. Katie could hardly believe that this was her teacher. Usually, Mrs. Derkman wore dresses and high heels. Her hair was always perfect, and she smelled like sweet perfume.

But today, Mrs. Derkman was a mess! She was wearing sweatpants and sneakers. Her hair was covered by a huge, floppy hat. Worst of all, she smelled like bug spray.

"Whoa! Check out Mrs. Derkman!" Kevin shouted. "She looks like a regular person."

A tall man with a beard and moustache walked over to Mrs. Derkman. "Here are your bags, honey," he said. "Your suitcase is so heavy. What do you have in there?"

"Bug spray, bug candles, and bug cream," Mrs. Derkman answered. "Those creatures aren't getting anywhere near me this year!"

"Did you hear him?" Kevin whispered to Katie. "He called Mrs. Derkman *honey*."

"That must be Mr. Derkman," Katie's mom said to Mrs. Fox. "He seems very nice."

Katie gasped. *Mrs. Derkman's husband?*

"We'd better go now," Mrs. Derkman said,

nervously looking at her watch.

Mr. Derkman smiled. "See you in three days," he said. "Don't let the bedbugs bite!"

Mrs. Derkman's eyes bulged. "Don't say that!" she squawked. Then she kissed her husband on the cheek.

The kids stared at their teacher in amazement.

"Okay, class, let's get on the bus!" Mrs. Derkman ordered her class. "We have no time to waste."

Katie sighed. Mrs. Derkman still *sounded* like herself.

"Well, this is it, sweetie," said Katie's mom. "Better get on line."

"You'll stay until the bus leaves?" Katie asked nervously.

Her mom nodded. "Of course, honey."

Katie gave Pepper one last pat, and then headed toward the bus. But before she could get on board, Manny started to yell.

"Mrs. Derkman, we can't leave!" He shouted out. "George isn't here yet!"

The kids all looked around. Where could George Brennan be?

Chapter 2

"Please, Mrs. Derkman, we have to wait!" Manny begged as the class began to board the bus. "Camp won't be fun without George!"

"We still have a few minutes before all the luggage is loaded onto the bus," Mrs. Derkman assured him. "I'm sure George will be here by then."

Katie found a seat near the window in the middle of the bus. Suzanne hopped into the seat beside her.

"Do you think George is coming?" Katie asked Suzanne as the girls buckled their seat belts.

"I won't miss him if he doesn't. George is

always telling dumb jokes," Suzanne said.

Katie frowned. Sometimes Suzanne could be pretty mean. Katie liked George's jokes. They were really funny. She liked George, too. He was the one who had given Katie her extremely cool nickname—Katie Kazoo.

"I hope we don't have to wait around all day for him," Jeremy said, as he took the seat across the aisle from Katie and Suzanne. "I want to get to camp!"

"There he is!" Kevin's voice rang out from the back of the bus. "Hurry up, George!" he shouted through the open window.

But George wasn't hurrying. In fact, it looked as though his dad was dragging him across the playground to the bus. George had a very angry scowl on his face.

Mr. Brennan marched George straight up to the yellow bus. "Have a good time, son," Mr. Brennan said.

"Fat chance," George barked back.

Mr. Brennan sighed. "It's just a few days at

Science Camp, George. It's not like you're joining the army."

George didn't answer. He walked to the back of the bus and plopped down in the seat across from Manny and Kevin.

Kevin smiled at his pal. "Am I glad to see you. You wouldn't believe the amazing things I snuck into my suitcase." Kevin leaned over to whisper in George's ear. "I packed all kinds of practical joke stuff—plastic bugs, pepper gum, and a whoopee cushion."

Usually, George was really into things like whoopee cushions. But not today. He just sat there, staring out the window with his hands crossed over his chest. "Big deal," he muttered.

Kevin looked surprised. "Come on. We're going to have so much fun!"

George shook his head. "No we're not. This whole Science Camp thing is dumb."

Jeremy looked back at him. "You're nuts, George. Camp's the best. "I should know.

I went to camp last summer."

Suzanne sighed. "You've only told us that about a million times."

"Well, I don't think camp's cool," George argued. "Who wants to go to camp when you can sleep in your own bed and have cable TV?"

As the bus drove away, Katie looked out the window and watched her mother become smaller and smaller. Soon, Katie couldn't see her mom at all. A really lonely feeling came over her.

Katie wasn't the only one feeling sad. Katie could see a tear falling down the side of Suzanne's face.

"Hey, you want to share a bunk bed?" Katie asked, trying to cheer her pal.

Suzanne smiled . . . a little. "Can I have the top?"

"Sure."

Jeremy turned to Katie and Suzanne. "You guys want to hear a camp cheer?" he asked.

"Why not?" Suzanne said.

Jeremy smiled broadly as he began to cheer.
"Brrr. It's cold in here. There must be 3A in
the atmosphere. All hands clap. All feet stamp.
We're the coolest kids at Science Camp!"

Soon the kids in class 3A were shouting Jeremy's cheer. Mandy Banks and Miriam Chan were even doing a hand-clapping game to the rhythm. Everyone was having fun.

Everyone except George. He looked miserable.

Katie joined in. She felt a little bit better. As Katie looked over at Jeremy's smiling face, she hoped that she would be as happy at camp as he'd been.

But Katie couldn't help feeling that something awful was going to happen at Science Camp.

Chapter 3

As the bus turned a corner, the kids caught a glimpse of the camp sign. Suddenly, everyone seemed to be talking at once.

Everyone but George, that is. He sat there like a lump.

"We're here, because we're here, because we're here, because we're here . . . " Jeremy began singing another one of his camp songs.

"Ooh, are those the cabins?" Mandy asked, pointing to the tiny little wooden huts that dotted the campgrounds.

"Did you see that lake?" Zoe added. "It's so blue."

"I wonder where the nature shack is,"

Manny said. "Mrs. Derkman told me they have goats and sheep there."

"Do you think they have full-length mirrors in the cabins?" Suzanne asked.

Before Katie could answer, the bus rolled to a stop. Immediately, the kids unbuckled their belts and bolted for the door.

One by one the children filed off the bus. Katie looked around. Science Camp was really pretty. The trees were blossoming. She could hear birds singing in the distance. And there was a clean smell to the breeze that circled gently around her head.

The breeze!

Suddenly Katie had a nervous feeling in the pit of her stomach.

Quickly she looked at her classmates. Their hair was blowing in the wind, too.

She stared at the trees. The leaves and blossoms were moving. *Phew*. It was just a normal, everyday breeze. For a moment there, Katie had been afraid that the *magic wind*

had followed her all the way to Science Camp.

The magic wind was a tornado-like wind that twisted and turned—but only around Katie. It was really scary. But the scariest part happened after the wind *stopped* blowing. That's when Katie turned into someone else!

It all started one really awful day. Katie had ruined her favorite jeans and burped in front of the whole class. That had been so embarrassing. Katie had wished that she could be anyone but herself.

There must have been a shooting star flying overhead or something when she made that wish, because the very next day, the magic wind blew, turning Katie into Speedy, the class hamster! Katie had spent a whole morning gnawing on wooden chew sticks and running on a hamster wheel.

Luckily, Katie had changed back into herself before anyone stepped on her!

Katie never knew who the magic wind might turn her into next. Already it had switcherooed her into the school lunch lady, Lucille, and the principal, Mr. Kane. And once the magic wind turned Katie into *Jeremy*. What a mess that had been!

Katie never knew when the magic wind was coming. She just hoped that the wind wouldn't be able to find her at Science Camp. It was going to be hard enough being away from home. She didn't want to have to be away from her body, too.

Chapter 4

Manny, George, and Kevin were all huddled together on the grass behind the bus. Manny and Kevin were whispering to each other and giggling. George just looked bored.

Finally, Manny walked up to Mrs. Derkman and stared at her arm. At first, he didn't say anything. Then he asked her, "Mrs. Derkman, what's black and green, has six legs, a furry body, and two antennae?"

Mrs. Derkman shrugged. "I don't know, Manny."

"I don't know either, but it's crawling up your arm!" Manny told her.

"*Aaaahhhhhh!*" Mrs. Derkman screamed

so loud, Katie was sure they could hear her back at Cherrydale Elementary School. The teacher jumped up and down, slapping her arm. "Get it off me! Get it off me right now!"

Suddenly, a woman with a deep, booming voice came up behind Mrs. Derkman. "What is going on here?" she demanded.

Katie gasped. The woman was very tall. Her muscles were bulging out of her green army uniform. She looked like she never smiled . . . ever. She seemed scarier than any bug.

"Th-th-there's a hairy bug on my arm," Mrs. Derkman stammered.

"Oh, give me a break," the woman in the army uniform barked. "Bugs are part of life out here. Get used to it, soldier."

Soldier?

Mrs. Derkman looked at her curiously. "Excuse me?" she asked.

"Um . . . I mean, there's nothing on your arm," the woman said.

Mrs. Derkman glanced at her bugless arm and sighed. "George Brennan, come here!"

George moped his way over toward the teacher. "I didn't do anything," he insisted.

"Maybe not. But I have a feeling that was your idea of a joke," Mrs. Derkman said.

"It wasn't. Honest," George insisted.

"I wouldn't worry about any more jokes." The woman in the uniform assured Mrs. Derkman. "I'm Genie Manzini, the head counselor. I don't allow for any joking at Science Camp." Genie glared at George.

"Maybe we should call her Genie the *Meanie*," Suzanne whispered to Katie.

Katie wanted to laugh, but she didn't dare. Who knew what Genie the Meanie might do?

"Okay troops . . . I mean, *boys and girls*," Genie corrected herself. "I want you to meet the staff. To begin with, I am the head counselor. *Everyone* here answers to me."

The children all turned around to see what Mrs. Derkman would say to that. Mrs. Derkman didn't like answering to anyone.

But Mrs. Derkman didn't seem to have heard anything Genie had said. She was too busy spraying herself with bug spray. "Get off me, you miserable ant!" The teacher muttered as she sprayed her sneaker.

Genie pointed to a small woman with short brown hair and a cheery smile. "This is Tess," she said. "She runs our animal program."

"Hi everyone," Tess greeted them. "I hope you will all visit the nature shack and help with the animals."

Katie grinned. Tess seemed nice. And maybe visiting the animals in the nature shack would keep her from missing Pepper so much.

"And this is Carson, our nature arts instructor," Genie said, pointing to a tall, thin man wearing sunglasses and a tie-dyed T-shirt.

"You won't believe all the things we can create with nature's art supplies," Carson told them. "We're going to have fun here, right?"

"Right!" the kids shouted back.

Genie did not look pleased.

Just then, a loud bell rang out over the campground. "Okay, that means chow time,"

Genie told them. "You have exactly twenty-seven minutes for lunch. Now line up."

The kids formed a straight line.

"March," Genie ordered. "Hup, two, three, four. Hup, two, three . . . "

As Katie marched toward the mess hall, she remembered what George's father had said about Science Camp not being the army.

Mr. Brennan couldn't have been more wrong.

Chapter 5

Genie the Meanie kept the kids moving all day long. They went from morning to night without a rest. Some of the activities—like making beeswax candles and feeding the animals—were kind of fun.

But Genie never once let the kids forget that Science Camp was part of school. She made them carry notebooks and pencils everywhere, so they could take notes on what they learned.

"I'm exhausted," Katie said as she flopped down on the bottom bunk.

"All I know is Science Camp made me really tired," Miriam added. "I think I could fall asleep anywhere. Even on this lumpy bed."

Suzanne put her foot on the metal edge of Katie's bed and hopped up onto her top bunk.

The top bunk sagged slightly over Katie's head. The sagging lump moved back and forth as Suzanne found a comfortable spot to lie down. For a minute, Katie thought the bed might come down on top of her.

It was easier not to look up, so instead Katie looked around the cabin. There were four bunk beds lined up along the walls. The walls of the cabin were made of pine-colored wood paneling. There were four screened-in windows on each wall.

Just then, the cabin door swung open. "Okay, girls, it's time for lights out," Tess said, as she walked in and flicked off the light.

As Tess left the cabin, Katie felt scared . . . and lonely. Pepper always slept on her bed with her at home. Now she was all alone.

Suddenly, Katie heard leaves rustling outside the bunk. "Suzanne," she whispered.

"Do you hear that?"

Suzanne listened for a second. "I think there's someone out there."

"Someone or some*thing*," Miriam suggested nervously.

Zoe leaped out of her bed and ran over to

where Katie was sleeping. "Do you mind if I just sit here?" she asked Katie. "I don't think I want to be so close to the door."

The crunching of the leaves was louder now. Whatever was out there was getting closer.

"Do you think it's a bear?" Katie asked.

"Maybe it's a monster," Mandy suggested. "A monster who hates kids at Science Camp."

Suddenly, a huge light beam came shining in through the cabin window.

"*Aaaaaaaaaahhhhhhhhh!*" The girls all screamed. "It's the Science Camp monster!"

But the light wasn't coming from a monster. It was coming from Genie the Meanie's flashlight.

"All right, boys, I see you out there," Genie shouted. "You've been bunkhopping!"

The girls all raced to the windows to see what was happening. In the glare of Genie's light, they could see Kevin and Manny's faces.

"I've got the perfect punishment for you two," Genie assured them in a voice that made the boys shake.

The head counselor grabbed Manny by the hand and walked him over to a huge old pine tree. "Hug it!" Genie ordered.

"Hug what?" Manny asked.

"The tree. *Hug the tree,*" Genie ordered again. She turned to Kevin. "You hug the one next to it. That way I can be sure you boys aren't going anywhere."

Kevin had no choice. He reached out his arms and hugged the tree. Manny did the same.

The girls knew they were supposed to be quiet after lights out. But they couldn't help it. The sight of Manny and Kevin hugging trees was just too funny. They all started to laugh.

And Genie the Meanie didn't tell them to stop.

Chapter 6

"What's that sticky stuff in your hair?" Carson asked Kevin, as everyone entered the mess hall for breakfast the next morning.

"Pine sap," Kevin replied.

"How'd you get that on your head?" the nature arts counselor asked.

Kevin moaned and tried to wipe his hair. "I don't want to talk about it."

Kevin took his tray and sat down beside Katie, Jeremy, Suzanne, and Manny.

"What's up with George?" Suzanne asked Kevin. "I thought you guys always sat together."

It was true. George, Manny, and Kevin

usually did everything together.

But today, George was sitting all by himself in the back of the mess hall. He looked miserable.

"I don't know what his problem is," Manny said. "He doesn't want to do anything. Like last night. We were all telling ghost stories in the cabin. George went to sleep!'"

"That doesn't sound like George," Katie agreed. "He loves scary stuff."

"So, Jeremy, when exactly is this place going to get fun?" Suzanne asked, changing the subject. "You keep talking about how great camp is, but I think Science Camp is a real drag."

Jeremy nodded. "This isn't like the camp I went to last summer," he agreed. "But maybe today we'll get to to play some games or something."

Just then, Genie passed by the table. Jeremy smiled nervously in her direction. "Excuse me, Genie."

The head counselor glared down at him. "What is it soldier . . . I mean *student?*"

"Are we going to have some free time today?" Jeremy asked. "Maybe we can play soccer or basketball or something. You know, have a little fun."

Genie's eyes opened wide. "This is not summer camp!" she shouted. "This is Science Camp. You are not here to play. You are here to learn. And nobody said learning has to be fun!"

Jeremy gulped. Genie sure sounded mad.

"I have a full schedule for you kids," she continued. "It begins with inspection. I'm going to check each of your cabins for neatness. And your beds had better be made well. I want those sheets pulled so tight I can bounce a quarter off them!"

"What does bouncing quarters on beds have to do with science?" Manny wondered aloud, after Genie walked away.

As the kids chowed down on their eggs,

Katie glanced over at George. He seemed very quiet. She was worried about him. Finally, she got up and walked over to sit beside her friend.

"Hey, George," Katie greeted him.

George didn't say anything. He just shoved a forkful of eggs into his mouth. "These are gross," he muttered between bites.

"I know egg-zactly what you mean," Katie joked.

George didn't laugh. Instead, he took another forkful of eggs.

"Are you looking forward to our hike this afternoon?" Katie asked, changing the subject.

George rolled his eyes. "No," he snapped. "Hikes are dumb. Everything here is dumb."

"George, why are you being so mean?"

"I'm not being mean. I'm just too cool for this place," George told her. "Can I help it if you're not?"

Katie's face got red. "That was a mean

thing to say, George Brennan!" she shouted. "I don't think you're cool at all. I think you're a jerk!"

Then, Katie got up and stormed out of the mess hall—before Mrs. Derkman had a chance to tell her that *jerk* isn't a word you use in school.

Chapter 7

After Genie had inspected their cabins, the kids in 3A gathered on the main lawn to get ready for their hikes. They each had their own water bottles and a bag of cookout food to carry.

Cookie, the camp cook, smiled at Katie as she handed her a bag. "There's no meat in yours," she assured Katie. Cookie knew that Katie was a vegetarian. "But I added extra carrot sticks and potato chips. I don't let kids go hungry."

"Thanks," Katie said with a grin.

The class had been split into small groups for their hikes. Katie, Suzanne, Jeremy and

George were in the same group.

"Who's our leader, anyway?" George asked. "Mrs. Derkman," Suzanne said.

Katie frowned. " I was hoping Tess or Carson could be our leader."

Just then Genie walked toward Katie and her friends. "Mrs. Derkman has a bad case of poison ivy," she told them. "She fell in a patch of it while running away from an oncoming fly. I'll be taking you on your hike.

"Okay, troops. March," Genie ordered. "Left, right, left, right."

Katie got in line behind George. He was going very slowly. "You'd better march faster," Katie told him. "Genie the Meanie is going to yell at you."

George reached into his pocket and pulled out a hard candy wrapped in shiny paper. "What's the hurry?" he mumbled as he sucked on the candy. "It's not like we're going any-where. It's a hike to nowhere."

"We're supposed to be looking at the

plants and animals in the woods," Katie reminded him. "See, there's a chipmunk." George was not impressed.

After they'd been hiking for a while, Katie marched up to the front of the line. "Genie," she asked quietly. "Are we anywhere near a bathroom?"

Genie pointed out into the woods.

"Behind that tree. Or that tree. Or any tree," Genie told her.

Katie gulped. "You mean I have to pee in the woods?"

Genie nodded. "Or hold it in."

That settled it. Katie ran off in the direction of a huge oak tree surrounded by some high shrubs. She hoped the bushes would hide her.

Suddenly, Katie felt a cold breeze on the back of her neck. The light wind felt great after the long hike she'd been on . . .until Katie realized that the wind wasn't blowing anywhere but on her.

This was no ordinary wind. This was the magic wind!

Oh no, Katie thought. *Not here. Not in the middle of the woods!*

The magic wind began spinning faster and faster, all around Katie. She shut her eyes tightly, and tried not to cry. As the fierce tornado swirled, she held on to the tree. She struggled to keep her feet on the ground. The wind just kept getting more and more powerful.

And then it stopped.

Katie was afraid to open her eyes. What if the wind had blown her away. What if she was all alone in the middle of the forest?

But Katie was *not* alone. The other kids were right nearby.

As Katie opened her eyes, Jeremy stared up at her.

"Genie?" he asked. "Why are you hugging that tree?"

Chapter 8

Katie looked down at her feet. Instead of her own bright red sneakers, she saw Genie's hiking boots. And she was wearing army pants instead of jeans.

Katie had become Genie the Meanie!

Uh-oh. Genie was in charge of the hike. She was supposed to teach the kids to build a fire, cook the food, and find the way back to camp.

Katie didn't know how to do any of those things.

"Hey, what happened to Katie?" George asked. "She's been gone a long time."

Katie gulped. She knew exactly where Katie was. But how could she explain that to her friends?

"Katie!" Jeremy called into the woods.

There was no answer.

"Katie Kazoo, quit goofing around," George shouted.

Suzanne began to panic. "She's missing!"

"Relax, she didn't go far," Katie assured her. "I'm sure if we just sit here she'll come back."

Suzanne was so scared she forgot to be afraid of Genie the Meanie. "We can't just sit here!" she declared. "She's lost in the woods somewhere. We've got to look for her!"

Katie didn't know what to do do. The real Genie probably would have searched for her. That was her job—to keep everyone safe.

"All right. We'll look for your friend. But let's be sure to stick together. I don't want to lose any more of you," Katie said, trying to sound like the real Genie the Meanie.

As the kids wandered through the woods, searching for their missing friend, Katie tried her best to act like a real head counselor. It wasn't easy. Katie had never been out in the woods before.

The kids were starting to panic. Katie had to do something to calm them down. She decided to change the subject. That's what a real head counselor would do—get the kids thinking about something else.

Katie pointed to a patch of leaves on the ground. Each of the green leaves had three parts. "Look at that beautiful plant," Katie said. She bent down to pick up a leaf.

"Genie, don't touch that!" Jeremy shouted. "That's poison ivy."

Oops! Katie gulped. What a mistake that would have been.

"Very good, Jeremy," Katie said. "I *meant* to do that. It was a test. I wanted to see if you kids could recognize poison ivy."

"I don't want to look at leaves," Suzanne

moaned. "I want to look for Katie."

"Or what's left of Katie," George added.

"Cut that out, George!" Suzanne shouted.

"Make me!" George screamed back.

Katie leaped between them. "Let's just keep walking," she ordered.

"Which way?" George groaned.

Katie led the kids down a dirt path. "Maybe she headed east," Katie told the kids. "We'll try that way."

"Uh, Genie," Jeremy interrupted, as Katie turned to her right. "We're actually heading west."

"How do you know?" Katie asked him.

"It's almost sunset. The sun sets in the west. It's in front of us right now."

Katie sighed. She didn't know any of this stuff. "Of course," Katie said. "I meant west. We'll head west."

"It's getting kind of dark," Suzanne moaned, as the kids walked behind Katie.

"That's just a cloud over the sun," Katie

assured her, trying to sound confident.

"Actually, I think it's getting dark because it's about six o'clock," Jeremy told her. "It'll be night soon."

"Oh, no!" Suzanne shouted. "Katie will be all alone in the woods at night!"

"Relax, Suzanne," Katie said. "We'll find your friend."

"Katie's not just any friend," Suzanne said. "She's my best friend. I'm worried about her." She looked at George and Jeremy. "Which is more than I can say for some people."

"Hey, she's my best friend, too," Jeremy argued.

"But you don't sound very worried," Suzanne told him.

"I am too worried," Jeremy said.

Katie sighed. "Please stop . . .Whoa!" Before Katie could finish her sentence, she went sliding down a long, slippery slope. When she reached the bottom, she found herself waist deep in thick, gooey mud!

"*Help!* Quicksand!" Katie shouted out. She looked up at George, Jeremy, and Suzanne. "I'm sinking! Help me!"

George stared down at the head counselor. "I'm not helping her," he told Jeremy and Suzanne. "Let the quicksand swallow her up."

"But she's the only one who knows the way back to camp!" Suzanne declared. "And now she's sinking into quicksand!"

"She's not sinking," Jeremy assured her. "And that's not quicksand. It's just a mudslide. We played on one of those at my summer camp. Genie, just grab on to that tree branch and pull yourself back up the hill." Katie did as she was told. She grabbed on to a low-lying branch and tried to pull herself up. It wasn't easy. The mud had made her hands slippery, and the hill was steep.

"Whoa!" Katie cried out, as she slipped back down the mudslide. She fell backward, tripped over a rock, and went rolling into the woods.

Finally, she landed in a thick pile of leaves. Frantically, Katie tried to find a path back up the hill. But there was mud every-where. Every time she tried to move up the hill, she'd slide back down.

And then, suddenly, she felt a familiar breeze hit the back of her neck.

The magic wind was back!

Wild tornado-like gusts swirled all around Katie's body. She grasped at a nearby tree, but it was out of her reach.

Bam! The strong wind knocked Katie off her feet. She fell to the ground with a *thud.* The wind was the fiercest it had ever been. Katie grabbed on to a huge rock. Her feet flew up in the air, but she refused to let go of that rock. She held on tightly.

And then the wind stopped.

Everything around her was perfectly calm.

Everything except Genie the Meanie, that is. She was lying on the ground, clutching a rock. And she wasn't at all

sure how she'd gotten there.

Genie looked down at her clothes. Her army pants were covered with mud. "What happened? What's going on here?" Genie barked to Katie, who was now standing beside her.

Katie knew she had to say something. "I'm so glad you found me," she blurted out. "I've been lost so long. You're a great counselor, Genie."

"*Head* counselor," Genie reminded her. She scrambled to her feet. Then she looked at Katie curiously. "You were lost?" she asked.

Katie grinned. "Of course. How else could you have found me?"

Chapter 9

"Okay, soldier, just another few feet," Genie shouted back to Katie. "Try to climb at the same time I do." Genie had wrapped her belt around Katie's waist. She was using the belt to tow Katie up the slippery hill.

Katie planted her feet firmly into the mud and tried to climb. "This is hard," she moaned.

"Almost there," Genie assured her.

"Hey, look," George cried out. "It's Katie Kazoo!"

As Katie and Genie wandered back toward the others, Jeremy raced over to them. "Where were you?" he demanded.

"I went into the woods to . . .to . . ."

"She went to pee." George giggled.

Katie blushed. "Anyway, I got lost, and Genie found me."

"Just in time," George said. "I'm starving. We never got to have our cookout because we were looking for you. Let's just get back to camp and eat something."

"Which way do we go?" Jeremy asked.

Genie's eyes confidently scanned the trees. Suddenly, her face fell. "Where are the red ribbons?" she muttered.

"What ribbons?" Katie asked.

"The red ribbons!" Genie exclaimed, sounding very nervous. "The ones that are tied to the trees. They mark the path back to camp."

"We must have wandered off the path when we were looking for Katie," Jeremy thought aloud. "Can't we take another path?"

"We could," Genie agreed, "if I knew one. But I have no idea how far we are from camp or which way to turn to go back. I'm not even sure how we got here. It's all sort of a blur."

"This is all your fault, Katie Kazoo," George snapped.

Katie stared at George. Did he know that it was she, not Genie, who had gotten them lost? Did George know about magic wind?

"If you hadn't disappeared, we wouldn't have had to look for you," George continued.

Okay, so George didn't know about the magic wind. But he was right. She was the reason the kids were lost. And now even Genie couldn't get them back safely.

"I hate the dark. I hate it," Suzanne blubbered. "We don't even have a flashlight."

"What if there really is a Science Camp monster out there? He could get us." George's eyes grew big. His lip quivered, but he didn't cry. He just stared out into the woods.

Even Jeremy seemed nervous. "Do you think the other kids in our class are worried about us?" he asked.

"Maybe they'll call the police to come look for us," Suzanne said.

"I'll bet Mrs. Derkman is a total wreck," George added. "You know how she can get."

"I doubt it," Katie said. "I'll bet she's fine. She knows we're with the head counselor. Genie can take care of us."

Hoot!

"What was that?" Genie cried out.

Katie gulped. Maybe Genie wouldn't be able to take care of them after all. It seemed that even the head counselor was scared to be in the woods at night.

"I think it was an owl," Katie told her. "Tess said there were a lot of owls in these woods. Don't worry, owls won't hurt you."

Grrrr. Just then, everyone heard a loud grumbling noise.

"Now what was *that?*" Genie wailed.

Katie giggled. "George's stomach."

"It always makes that noise when I'm hungry," George moaned.

"Well, we still have all our cookout supplies," Jeremy suggested. "We could eat. All we have to do is build a fire."

"I don't know how," Suzanne said. "My dad always does the grilling at our house."

The kids looked to Genie for help, but the head counselor was busy staring into the woods. "Where are those ribbons?" she kept saying over and over. "I need my ribbons."

"We're going to have to do this ourselves," Katie told her friends. She was trying to act like a head counselor. After all, she'd been Genie—for a little while, anyway. "Jeremy, did they teach you to make a fire at your camp?"

Jeremy nodded. "I can build one. But we're not allowed to use matches, remember?"

"Genie can handle that," Katie said. "You just tell us how to do the rest."

Jeremy pointed to some fallen branches nearby. "Suzanne, you and Katie go collect sticks. Start with little twigs, and then get bigger ones. Make sure the wood is dry.

George, you and I will get some wood, too."

Before long, the kids had plenty of wood. Jeremy showed them how to build a little box of twigs. Genie lit the twigs with her matches. Then she and Jeremy built up the fire, by throwing logs onto the flames.

There was plenty of food to cook. Jeremy, Suzanne, and George cooked hot dogs on

sticks. Katie ate carrot sticks and potato chips. Then the kids toasted marshmallows.

Genie didn't eat anything. She just sat by the fire, staring into the woods.

When the kids were finished with their food, Katie turned to Genie. "We should put the fire out, right?" she asked.

Genie nodded. She seemed to have finally calmed down. At least she wasn't mumbling about the red ribbons anymore. "We shouldn't leave it burning while we sleep," she told Katie.

"Sleep?" Suzanne asked. "Sleep where?"

Genie emptied her canteen of water on the fire. Katie and Jeremy did the same. "We're going to have to sleep here tonight," Genie told the kids, as the last of the flames disappeared. It was dark now. The moon was the only light they had.

"Sleep on the hard ground?" Suzanne asked. "With all that dirt?"

"What's the matter?" Jeremy asked her.

"You didn't bring the right clothes for sleeping outside?"

Suzanne made a face, but didn't say anything.

Katie grabbed a paper garbage bag and began filling it with soft leaves.

"What are you doing?" Suzanne asked her.

"Making a pillow," she answered.

That seemed like a good idea. The kids all grabbed bags and began to make their own pillows. Katie made an extra one for Genie. She felt bad for her. None of this had really been her fault.

Katie yawned. Her eyes were feeling heavy. She lay down and put her head on her pillow. Before she knew what was happening, Katie was asleep.

Chapter 10

Katie hadn't been asleep very long when she heard footsteps in the woods. There was someone prowling around the campsite!

Katie looked at Genie. She was curled up in a ball, snoring away. She wasn't going to be any help.

Now a quiet sniffling noise was coming from where the fire had been.

Slowly, Katie stood and walked in the direction of the sniffles.

There was George. He was wide awake—and he'd been crying.

"George, what's wrong?" she asked him.

George wiped his nose with his sleeve.

"Nothing," he mumbled.

"Come on, George," Katie urged. "I know something's wrong."

"You're gonna laugh" he said quietly.

"No, I won't. I promise."

"I'm scared," George whispered. "I've never been away from home before."

Katie understood that feeling perfectly. Now she knew why George had acted so

grumpy. He didn't want anyone to know.

"You won't tell, will you?" he begged.

"Never." Katie looked around. Everyone else was sleeping. "I have a great idea. Let's stay up all night and see the sun rise.

George smiled a little. "We can tell jokes and stories and stuff."

"Okay," Katie agreed. "Want to see a neat trick?" She put on the hood of her sweatshirt. Then she pulled the strings really tight so the hood closed around her face.

"That's funny," George said. "You look like a faceless monster."

"A faceless Science Camp monster," Katie giggled.

"Do you know what fairy tale gives a monster the shivers?" George asked her.

Katie shook her head.

"Ghoul-dilocks and the Three Brrrrs!" he laughed at his own joke.

Katie grinned. George was back to normal. One problem solved.

Chapter 11

The next morning, the group was up early. They wanted to get back to camp right away.

"Can you find the right path now?" Jeremy asked Genie hopefully.

"I'm not sure," she replied.

Katie could tell that her friends were getting scared again. But somehow, things seemed less frightening in the sunlight.

"I'm hungry," George moaned. "Do we have any food left from last night? Maybe a hot dog or something?"

Suzanne made a face. "Hot dogs for breakfast? Yuck!"

"I'll eat anything when I'm this starved," George told her.

Katie checked the food pack. It was empty. "We don't have any food left,"

George looked upset. Then, suddenly, he brightened. "Yes, we do," he said. "I have those candies I brought on the hike."

At first Genie seemed angry. "You brought candy on the hike?" Then her stomach growled. "I'll take one," she added.

George reached into his pocket. Then he frowned as he pulled out an empty hand. "This is terrible!"

"What?" Katie asked. "Did you finish them all?"

George shook his head. "There's a hole in my pocket. The candies fell out."

"Oh, no!" Jeremy moaned. "That's awful."

Just then, Katie spotted a shiny round object over by a tree. A few feet away she saw another one . . . and then another. Katie raced over and picked up one of the shiny things.

"It's not awful at all," she told the others.

"George just saved us!"

"How did I do that?" he asked her.

"These are your candies," Katie told him, holding up a shiny wrapped treat. "They must have been falling out of your pocket the whole time we were hiking. All we have to do is follow the trail of candies. They'll lead us back to camp. And we can eat as we hike," she added, popping a butterscotch into her mouth.

Chapter 12

The tired hikers arrived back at camp before their friends woke up. In fact, the whole camp was still asleep—except for Cookie. She was waiting for them outside the Mess Hall.

"Where have you all been?" she asked, as Genie and the kids walked onto the camp-grounds. "I was up all night worrying. If you didn't come back soon, I was going to have send out a search party."

"It's a long story," Genie told Cookie.

"We got lost. We slept in the woods. And now we're back," Jeremy explained.

"Well, it's sure good to see you," Cookie told them. "Why don't you all take showers? Then

I'll make you a special treat for breakfast. You look starved."

That sounded great to Katie. She was really hungry.

"There's something else I have to do first," George said, as he ran off in the direction of the cabins.

"You know, that was actually kind of fun," Jeremy told Katie and Suzanne as they walked.

"Wait until the other kids hear what a wimp Genie turned out to be!" Suzanne laughed.

Katie shook her head. "I don't think we should tell the other kids about that. It's not nice to make fun of her for being scared."

"But she acted so tough before . . ." Suzanne began.

"She was just doing her job," Katie told her. "She had to be tough. It's a lot of responsibility being a head counselor. You're in charge of everything."

Before Suzanne could argue, the kids heard a loud scream coming from one of the cabins.

"*Spider. . . on my pillow!*"

Mrs. Derkman came racing out of her cabin. Her face was dotted with big blobs of pink lotion. Her hair was wrapped up in curlers. She was wearing a polka-dot flannel nightgown and a pair of fuzzy yellow slippers. She looked awful.

"Wow, check out Mrs. Derkman!" Suzanne exclaimed.

"Oh, no!" Katie gasped.

Jeremy couldn't say anything. He was laughing too hard.

As Mrs. Derkman stood in the middle of the campground screaming, George snuck out of her cabin with a big smile on his face. He ran off before the teacher could spot him.

Katie glanced at Genie. She was looking right in the direction of Mrs. Derkman's cabin. There was no way she could have missed seeing George run out of there.

Katie frowned. Was Genie going to punish George?

But Genie didn't yell or even call George over. Instead, she walked over to Katie and her friends, and laughed along with them.

Chapter 13

Katie was really sad when the time came to get on the bus and drive back to Cherrydale. Science Camp had been really fun. She was going to miss the bunnies in the nature shack and Cookie's chocolate-chip cookies.

But mostly Katie was going to miss Genie.

It turned out that the head counselor could be really nice when she wanted to. She taught the kids how to melt chocolate and marshmallows on graham crackers to make s'mores. And she showed them how to make beads out of clay that they dug from the ground.

"Maybe we can come back here again in fourth grade," Katie said to Suzanne, as they took seats in the back of the bus.

"That would be so cool," Suzanne agreed. "We could teach everyone how to build a fire."

Just then, Katie felt someone knocking on the window beside her. It was Genie.

Katie opened the window. "Thanks so much," she said. "I really learned a lot."

Genie grinned. "So did I. I learned that kids can do a whole lot for themselves . . . if you give them the chance."

As the bus drove off, Katie felt a cool breeze blow on her through the open window. She was pretty sure it wasn't a magic wind. But she reached up and shut the window— just in case.

No sense taking any chances.

Chapter 14

Science Camp definitely was a fun time. The nature arts counselor had lots of great ideas for nature projects the kids could do. Everyone in class 3A came home with natural soaps that they made all by themselves.

You can make your own Science Camp soap on a rope. Here's how.

Soap on a Rope
You will need:
3 cups Ivory Snow detergent or other
    soap flakes
bowl
liquid food coloring

1 cup water
vegetable oil
a thin piece of rope

Here's what you do: Pour the soap flakes into a bowl. Put a few drops of food coloring in the water. Pour the water onto the soap flakes. Use your hands to mix the contents of the bowl until they feel like clay or dough. Massage a drop or two of vegetable oil into the palms of your hands. Now shape the soap anyway you like. Tie the ends of the rope together. Gently push the knotted end of the rope into your finished soap shape. Let the soap stand overnight to set.